W9-BYH-753

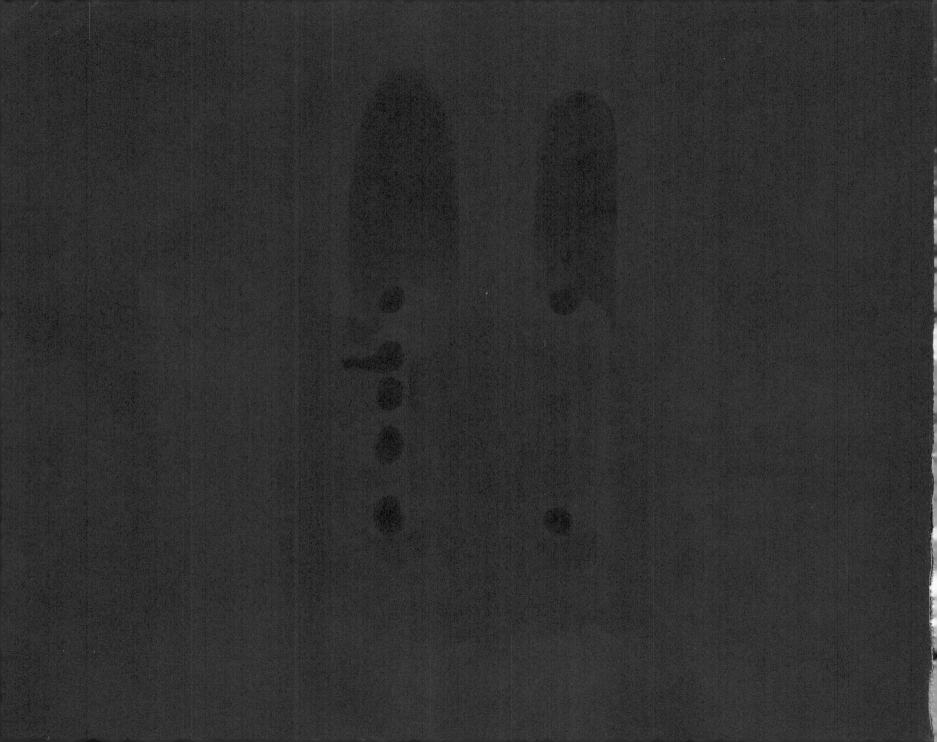

Geez Louise!

Susan Middleton Elya

illustrated by Eric Brace

G. P. PUTNAM'S SONS
NEW YORK

Library of Congress Cataloging-in-Publication
Data   Elya, Susan Middleton, 1955–
Geez Louise! / Susan Middleton Elya ;
illustrated by Eric Brace.   p. cm.
Summary: Louise the stinkbug must
face the bullying cockroach Kiki in
a skating contest.   [1. Insects—
Fiction. 2. Ice skating—Fiction.
3. Contests—Fiction.]
i. Brace, Eric, ill. ii. Title.
PZ8.3.E514 Gae 2003
[E]—dc21 00-068404
ISBN 0-399-23582-5
10 9 8 7 6 5 4 3 2 1
First impression

E
FICTION
ELY

unp. : #b. 11.

To my fellow writers: April, Bob, Gary, Joanna, Kathy, Katie, Marisa, Mary, Nancy, Rosie, Sue, Susie, Susan, and Teresa.   —S. M. E.

For the Bishop family . . . always making me feel like family too.   —E. B.

Louise the stinkbug was awfully stinky.
She could count her friends on her little pinky.

Everyone scattered when she passed them.
She didn't mean to, but she gassed them.

Termite Tara, who was almost blind,
ignored the smell, said she didn't mind.

The two went skating every day.
The other bugs all stayed away.

Then they heard about a contest coming—
a skating showdown. The town was humming.

But Louise knew a bug who just might beat her.
Her knees shook every time she'd meet her.

Kiki the roach was tough and mean.
Her boots were black; her eyes were green.

She scared the beetles
into bunches,
chased the fleas
and stole their lunches.

But the bug she really loved to tease
was the one who smelled the worst—Louise!

"Come on," said Tara, "you're first-rate.
 You have to take a stand and skate!

For every bug bugged by that bully,
 winged or wingless, smooth or woolly . . .

You've got to show that you can win."
 Louise thought hard. She rubbed her chin.

That roach was rotten, bad and sneaky.
 "I might," she said. "I don't like Kiki."

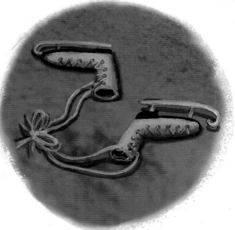

So Tara helped Louise get ready.
Her jumps looked clean. Her turns were steady.

SKaTeR's CHeCKLiST

CoRReCT

☑ FoRM
☑ LANDiNG
☑ SmiLe

OOPS!

☐ A
☐ L
☐ WiNG
EXTeNS

For weeks bugs buzzed, "Louise has guts."
On Contest Day they said, "She's nuts!"

BIG
★ SKATING ★
CONTEST
TODAY

first prize is
StiLL One LaRge
Shiny tROPhy

KiKi

Kiki showed up at half past three.
"You've got some nerve to challenge me!"

"I just can't do it," squeaked Louise.
"You've got to skate!" said Tara. "Please!"

Then Kiki came out in sequined garb.
She threw Louise another barb:

"Stinkbug loser,
I hate your stench!"
Louise's jaw began to clench.

If I could win, she thought, they'd see . . .
there's more than stinkiness to me.

"Who's first to skate?"
the announcer uttered.
"Me!" cried Louise.
The whole crowd shuddered.

Louise's heart went thump-thump-thump.
She started with her triple jump.

She launched herself into rotation,
achieved good height and spin formation.

She landed clean. There was a pause,
and then a roar of bug applause.

"She'll beat the bully!" an earwig cheered.
"That's nothing special," Kiki jeered.

Kiki began with her trademark spin.
It looked like the roach would surely win.

She glided smoothly on her toes,
passed Louise, and plugged her nose.

She stayed plugged for her triple jump
and fell onto her cockroach rump.

She knocked down bugs like bowling pins
and sideswiped Tara in the shins.

"Louise can't win! You'll see. Just wait."
But no more bugs stood up to skate.

"If no one else will join the fun,"
the announcer said,

"Louise
has
won!"

The bugs took Louise around the rink.
"You like me even though I stink?"

cLaP
cLaP
cLaP
cLaP
cLaP

To her surprise the other bugs
unplugged their noses and gave her hugs.

"Geez, Louise!" they said. "You're cheeky.
You stood up to that bully Kiki!"

Now Louise has friends galore—
she counts with fingers, toes, and more.

And the one who coached her to success?
Louise said, "Tara, you're the best!"